MARTHA, No!

Edward
Hardy

Deborah
Allwright

For all those who
try to say Yes
E.H.

To Molly
D.A.

JP

EGMONT
We bring stories to life

First published in Great Britain 2010
by Egmont UK Limited
239 Kensington High Street
London W8 6SA

Text copyright © Edward Hardy 2010
Illustrations copyright © Deborah Allwright 2010

The moral rights of the author and illustrator have been asserted

ISBN 978 14052 4078 9 (Hardback)
ISBN 978 14052 4911 9 (Paperback)

1 3 5 7 9 10 8 6 4 2

A CIP catalogue record for this title is available from the British Library

Printed and bound in Singapore

Visit Edward at www.kissyhuggra.com and Deborah at www.deborahallwright.com

Martha Felicity Molly-Anne May
has a *special surprise* on her doorstep today.

It's her sparkling new nanny,
Miss Harrington-Chive,
come to look after Martha
from nine until five.

Mother whispers, "I'm sure you'll be *perfect*, although there is something important I think you should know:

Nannies come to us once but then never again. Why, in this year alone we've already had ten!"

"Oh, don't fret," booms the woman –
"You've nothing to fear!

Nanny's looked after
hundreds of children, my dear!"

"As for Martha? Just look at her –
sweet, meek and mild –

Why, I've never met
quite so *angelic* a child!"

"Yes, an angel . . ." sighs Mother,
"but Nanny, you'll want to
watch out because angels
are hard to hold on to."

"What nonsense!" squawks Nanny.
"*Come on*, Martha May!
I won't tolerate dawdling
on such a fine day!"

So they set off together and walk hand in hand
to the square where they find a delightful brass band.

And then Martha hops on-stage
to have a quick blow . . .
"Oh my goodness!
Be *careful*, dear –

At the Science Museum, the guide says: "Before us,
we see the *magnificent* Tyrannosaurus!"

But Martha can't see much at all from below . . .
"Oh my goodness! Be *careful*, dear –

Half-past twelve, so it's time to have something to eat.
Nanny thinks that a pizza would make a nice treat.

Yes, but *whose* little hand
is that spinning the dough?

"Oh my goodness!
Be *careful*, dear –

MARTHA, NO!"

At the Gallery they study the Great Works of Art,
but of course, little Martha would rather take part.

And so crayons in hand and on tippety-toe . . .
"Oh my goodness! Be *careful*, dear –

At the playground, while Nanny does things with her wig,
in the sandpit a girl is beginning to dig . . .

How she flashes
her little blue spade to and fro . . .
"Oh my goodness! Be *careful*, dear –

At the tea-room, poor Nanny
is getting fed up
because Martha *insists*
she needs more than one cup.

But with
two and then
three cups,
her teacups
soon grow . . .

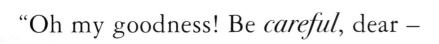

"Oh my goodness! Be *careful*, dear –

On a bench, Nanny sits
without saying a thing,
while nearby, Martha plays
with a long piece of string.

And then out of the blue
a warm breeze starts to blow . . .
And the string pulls her upwards
so gently and so . . .

Little Martha (oh, *my* . . .)
doesn't *think* to let go . . .

And poor Nanny
wakes up,
crying —

"NO! MARTHA . . ."

Until . . . **POP!**

and then . . . **POP!**

and then . . .

POP!

and then . . .

Martha

Felicity

Molly-Anne

May

makes a safe return home
at the end of her day.

"Oh my goodness!" gasps Mother.
"Why, Martha, it's *you*!
But where's Nanny? Don't tell me
we've lost *this* one too?

Well, *that's it* – no more nannies!
We'll just have to be
how we were at the start –
just my Martha and me.

We shall manage together,
though how, I can't guess.
Perhaps *you* know a way, dear . . ."

And Martha says, "*Yes.*"